Surprise Momma and Poppa...
I'm Coming
Down from *Heaven*

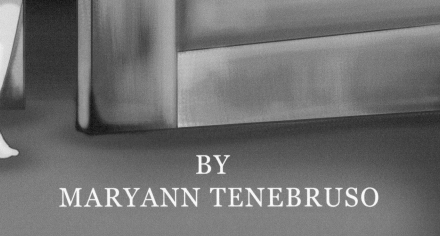

BY
MARYANN TENEBRUSO

To order additional copies of this book, contact:
Xlibris
844-714-8691
www.Xlibris.com
Orders@Xlibris.com

ISBN: 978-1-6698-7911-4 (sc)
ISBN: 978-1-6698-7910-7 (e)

Print information available on the last page

Rev. date: 05/26/2023

Surprise Momma and Poppa... I'm Coming Down from Heaven

By, MaryAnn Tenebruso

Dedicated to St. Peter's church in Pt. Pleasant Beach, New Jersey where I prayed in the morning and on Sundays. To Bryan's mom Jeanne Sullivan and husband Jim. To my two brother's Danny and Giancarlo, Also, to my parents Tina and Desi who are helping as grandparents to raise Luke. And my son's beloved father resting in heaven Bryan J. Harnik. And finally, to my late grandmother Anna Nicoletti may they rest in peace and watch over us as we think of them every day in our hearts.

4

West Long Branch, New Jersey is where my mom had many doctor's appointments for nine months to find out all about me on each visit. It is a small beach town where she delivered me at the hospital near the beach. Her doctor's appointment is where she and my dad found out on Valentine's Day that they were going to have a baby. She had a Lady Doctor named Jennifer show her pictures of me on an ultrasound machine. This is when she was so happy to hear my first heartbeat. My dad teared up they were so happy. They were young parents. My mom told my dad we are going to love this baby so much!

My mom and dad wanted to share this surprise with close family and friends. Soon it will change their lives forever. I will have a dad, grandparents, and an aunt and uncles too! My dad took my mom to an Italian restaurant in Brielle to celebrate the news.

Afterwards my mom called her best friend Rita and told her how excited they were. Rita was so surprised, she said, "Wow!" This was big news.

My mom's first thoughts were to pray to God for a healthy baby. My mom believes in prayer. My mom had many questions about me to ask God. She asked, how tall will I be? How much will I weigh? What color eyes will I have? What color hair will I have? And most importantly what day will my birthday be?

Mom gained weight all over. Jennifer her family doctor cared for my mom until I was going to come out into the world! They expected to have me on November 1st. My dad, grandpa, grandma, uncles and aunt guessed if I was a boy or a girl. But my mom told everyone she had a feeling she would be having a boy from the very beginning. Then, Nurse Gloria told mom it was a boy! That was her guess, and she was right! They played games and picked names from a hat. Their favorite names were Luke, London, and Marco. Dad considered naming me after his grandfather's Julian and James. But my mom knew my name from the start. They thought of how excited they would be to see me on my birthday. They wanted a boy!

Mom had to take care of herself spiritually and attend morning bible study at her church. She became very calm and welcoming of her new world as a mom. She stopped worrying about how she was dressed and how her hair and make-up looked. My grandma Tina comforted her with positive thoughts.

After her doctor's appointments were done, she learned to be happy. She read books to guide her and my dad to become new parents. They were showered with new gifts for my new nursery! She looked at parent magazines too for coupons on baby formula and ideas for what to put in her mother's bag to carry around for me.

Sometimes she could feel her belly move. It made her smile a lot! My mom felt little flurries, those were my feet kicking her. She felt them most in the center of her lower belly. She says every time she relaxed, went to church or ate she would feel me kick. I was most active at afternoon. She says it felt like I was happy and moving around. The best places to relax was in her room watching TV at night with dad and her dog Coco. She loved to go to church, exercise by going for a walk in the park. At the end of the day before going to bed, she would change into her pajamas. She watched her favorite shows on TV and inspirational movies. She read the bible a lot. She dreamed about everything! Mostly of meeting me!

My nursery theme was a circus. The colors they chose were primary colors like red, blue, orange, and green. My mom and dad set up a baby crib and changing table. And on the wall, they hung a cross in my room. They had toys waiting for me. A little lamb by G.U.N.D. A lion for tummy time and a little turkey for my first thanksgiving. In the car they have baby car keys, and fun sunshine toy that sings you are my sunshine.

Finally, my birthday was about to happen. My mom was tossing and turning and couldn't sleep. My parents grabbed their bag and drove to the hospital. On a very memorable day with the American flag waving in the air on a cloudy yet beautiful day I was born, in the morning on October 30th . They named me Luke Gabriel after an angel and sang la la la la . I weighed 7lbs 12 oz I was 19 inches long. I Had reddish brown hair with green eyes. My mom and dad said I was perfect, they loved me, they were so happy!

THE END

Printed in the United States
by Baker & Taylor Publisher Services